Published by Ladybird Books Ltd
80 Strand London WC2R 0RL
A Penguin Company
2 4 6 8 10 9 7 5 3 1
LADYBIRD and the device of a ladybird are trademarks of Ladybird Books Ltd
Copyright © 2003 Disney
Based on the Pooh stories by A.A.Milne
(Copyright the Pooh Properties Trust)

Printed in Italy
www.ladybird.co.uk

Disney

Piglet's
BIG
MOVIE

Deep in the Hundred-Acre Wood, Piglet was pasting pictures into his scrapbook. The drawings were of his friends – they reminded him of all the happy times they had shared together.

Just then, Piglet heard noises outside. He followed the sounds, and found that his friends had a Big Plan – they were going to harvest honey!

Rabbit was playing the violin, hoping to lure the bees out of their own hive and into a new hive the friends had made.

"Can I help with your Big Plan?" Piglet asked.

"Another time, when you're a bit of a bigger Piglet," said Tigger.

Suddenly the bees started swarming out – but they weren't going into the new hive. They were heading for Eeyore!

Piglet grabbed the megaphone that Eeyore had been using and bravely held it high. The bees buzzed straight through and into the new hive.

"Our plan worked!" said Rabbit.

No one had even noticed Piglet! He walked away, feeling very, very small.

As Piglet disappeared unnoticed, the honey harvesters were in trouble! The trapped bees had escaped and were buzzing furiously after the friends. Pooh and his gang ran, tumbling and crashing over each other and Pooh's honey pot.

"Let's make a beeline for Piglet's house!" Rabbit shouted.

Safe inside, they found Piglet's scrapbook – but no Piglet!

"Where can he be?" wondered Rabbit.

"Maybe his scrapbook will tell us," Pooh suggested. "It's filled with Piglet's memories – so maybe it remembers where Piglet is."

The first page had a picture of Owl's house.

"Let's look there," said Pooh.

Just as the friends set off to find *Piglet*, he was out in the woods looking for *them*! But when he went back to where he had left them, all Piglet found was a broken honey pot.

"Something must have happened to my friends!" he thought. "I may be small, but in the biggest, helpfullest way!"

Meanwhile, in another part of the wood, the gang realised that Piglet wasn't at Owl's house, so Pooh and the others decided to look at the scrapbook again.

Rabbit was looking at a picture of Kanga and Roo when they first came to the Hundred-Acre Wood.

The gang remembered how they were all scared of Kanga at first, but Piglet had been brave enough to get to know her. He even let her give him a bath!

"If it weren't for Piglet, we never would have found out how nice Kanga was," said Pooh.

The friends rushed to Kanga's house. She gave them some yummy cookies, and Roo joined the gang as they went off into the woods to search for Piglet again.

"So where do we look now?" Roo asked.

"The scrapbook will give us an idea," said Pooh, as he turned the page.

Roo was looking at a picture of the day he fell into the river. The gang had been worried about Roo being in the water on his own. Rabbit and Pooh wanted to rescue him – but it was Piglet who had used a big stick to save Roo and got him back safely to Kanga.

"But, nobody had said 'Hooray for Piglet'!" Roo remembered. "He was so brave. For someone so small."

It was starting to get very windy in the wood and the friends could hear thunder rumbling in the distance. Roo was worried about Piglet.

"Piglet shall be very all right indeed. Don't let his small size worry you," said Pooh.

"Yep," said Eeyore. "Once he even made a whole house!"

"Do you know the story of *The House at Pooh Corner,* Roo?" asked Pooh.

The friends told Roo how they couldn't get the house right and that it only got built when Piglet helped. Pooh sighed and wished they had called it *The House at Pooh and Piglet Corner.*

There was a sudden crash of thunder, and rain began to fall. Piglet's scrapbook got wet and soggy, and then a huge gust of wind blew it into the river! Soon the scrapbook, along with Piglet's memories, began to float downstream towards the waterfall.

But there was no time to think about the scrapbook. Roo was shivering, and the others didn't want him to catch a cold out in the storm. So they all went back to Piglet's house, where Rabbit made Roo a warming cup of tea.

The gang was safe and warm and dry, but they all knew someone was missing – and they wished he was there. Sighing, Pooh drew a picture of Piglet on the steamy window.

"That's the Piglet I know," said Pooh. "Always glad to see you."

"Always thoughtful," said Tigger.

"Always brave," added Rabbit.

"Never thinking of himself," said Eeyore.

Soon they were all drawing pictures of Piglet. And they knew they had to go out and find him, wherever he was.

Out in the storm, the friends searched everywhere, calling Piglet's name.

They didn't find Piglet – but they did find some pages from his scrapbook.

"If we can put Piglet's scrappitybook back together... " said Tigger.

" ...then we can find him in no time!" Pooh finished.

Soon they had collected lots of pages from Piglet's scrapbook. Then they found the main part of the book, it was hanging from a branch of an old tree trunk. Pooh went out after it, never thinking how much danger he was in – until he slipped off the tree trunk and got caught on a branch.

Pooh's friends grabbed hold of one another and made a 'rescue rope'.

"The rescue rope isn't rescuing!" shouted Pooh.

Who could help?

"Piglet!" everyone shouted, and there he was!

Piglet was nervous – but his friends needed him, and that made him brave.

"Hang on, Pooh!" he called.

Suddenly, with a terrible CRACK, the tree trunk broke. Pooh, Piglet and the tree trunk fell into the river and all vanished under the waterfall. The friends looked on and gasped in fear.

Fear turned to joy when Pooh and Piglet came rolling out of the hollow tree trunk, safe and sound.

"We're so glad to see you!" cried Tigger, bouncing Piglet in the air.

They told Piglet what had happened to his scrapbook.

"The scrapbook's not important," said Piglet.

Back home, looking at all the drawings, Piglet could hardly believe his eyes. He was filled with happiness – because he saw that, to his friends, he wasn't a small Piglet, but a very BIG Piglet, after all!